April & Mae
and the
Soccer Match

EVERY DAY
WITH
April & Mae

SUNDAY

April & Mae and the Tea Party

MONDAY

April & Mae and the Book Club Cake

TUESDAY

April & Mae and the Soccer Match

WEDNESDAY

April & Mae and the Talent Show

THURSDAY

April & Mae and the Animal Shelter

FRIDAY

April & Mae and the Sleepover

SATURDAY

April & Mae and the Movie Night

Collect them ALL!

April & Mae

and the

Soccer Match

THE TUESDAY BOOK

MEGAN DOWD LAMBERT

Illustrated by BRIANA DENGOUE

ini Charlesbridge

To my daughter Emilia, who loves soccer
and is a good friend. I love you and am so lucky
to be your mom.—M. D. L.

To my daughter, Bellarose.—B. D.

Text copyright © 2022 by Megan Dowd Lambert
Illustrations copyright © 2022 by Briana Arrington-Dengoue
All rights reserved, including the right of reproduction in whole
or in part in any form. Charlesbridge and colophon are registered
trademarks of Charlesbridge Publishing, Inc.

At the time of publication, all URLs printed in this book were
accurate and active. Charlesbridge, the author, and the illustrator are not
responsible for the content or accessibility of any website.

Published by Charlesbridge
9 Galen Street, Watertown, MA 02472 • (617) 926-0329 • www.charlesbridge.com

Library of Congress Cataloging-in-Publication Data
Names: Lambert, Megan Dowd, author. | Dengoue, Briana, illustrator.
Title: April & Mae and the soccer match: the Tuesday book / Megan Dowd
    Lambert; illustrated by Briana Dengoue.
Other titles: April and Mae and the soccer match
Description: Watertown, MA: Charlesbridge, 2022. | Series: Every day with
    April & Mae | Audience: Ages 5–8. | Summary: "April and Mae are best friends
    (and so are their pets). When Mae misses a soccer goal, April helps her realize
    that the fun is in playing, not winning."—Provided by publisher.
Identifiers: LCCN 2020050998 (print) | LCCN 2020050999 (ebook) |
    ISBN 9781580898881 (hardcover) | ISBN 9781632897589 (ebook)
Subjects: LCSH: Best friends—Juvenile fiction. | Soccer stories. | Disappointment—
    Juvenile fiction. | Pets—Juvenile fiction. | CYAC: Soccer—Fiction. |
    Disappointment—Fiction. | Best friends—Fiction. | Friendship—Fiction. |
    Pets—Fiction.
Classification: LCC PZ7.1.L26 An 2022 (print) | LCC PZ7.1.L26 (ebook) |
    DDC 813.6 [E]—dc23
LC record available at https://lccn.loc.gov/2020050998
LC ebook record available at https://lccn.loc.gov/2020050999

Printed in China
(hc) 10 9 8 7 6 5 4 3 2 1

Illustrations done in Photoshop
Illustrations colorized by Gisela Bohórquez
Display type set in Jacoby by Adobe
Text type set in Grenadine by Markanna Studios Inc.
Color separations and printing by 1010 Printing International Limited
    in Huizhou, Guangdong, China
Production supervision by Jennifer Most Delaney
Designed by Cathleen Schaad

April and Mae
play hard.

April loves to play
with her dog.
Mae loves to play
with her cat.
Mae is fast.
April is not.
April is bouncy.
Mae is not.

But April and Mae are friends.
Best friends.
And their pets
are best friends, too.

On Tuesdays,
April and Mae play soccer.

April likes to play.
Mae likes to win.
Mae likes to run.
April likes to cheer.
Their pets like to watch.
It is fun!

One Tuesday,
it rains before the match.
The field is muddy.
Soon the players are muddy, too.

The match is almost over.
Mae runs.
April cheers,
"Hey, hey!
Get out of the way!
Here . . .
comes . . .
Mae!"

Mae kicks the ball hard.
She slips!

She misses the goal.
She falls down in the mud.
The pets don't move in time.

The match ends.
April cheers,
"It's all right!
It's OK!
We will win
another day!"

Then April slips.
She falls down in the mud, too.
April laughs and laughs.

But Mae does not laugh.
The pets look sad.
April stops laughing.
This is not fun.

April and Mae
walk off the field.
"Are you OK?" asks April.

"No," says Mae.
"Look at me!"
April looks.

"Look at me!" says April.
Mae looks.

17

"Why are you happy?" asks Mae.
"We lost.
   And you are muddy, too."

"It was fun," says April.
"And I love mud."

"Well, I do not love mud," says Mae.
"And I missed the goal."

"But you tried," says April.

"I tried to *win*," says Mae.

April feels bad for her friend.
What can she do?

April and Mae go to Mae's house.
April sees the goodies Mae baked.
"You are the *best!*" says April.

Will that make Mae
feel glad again?

No, it does not.
Mae pouts.

"I am the best at baking," says Mae.

"But I am the worst at soccer."

"Hey," says April.

"Don't lie about my best friend!"

Mae smiles a small smile.

That makes April feel glad.

Then April and Mae
go to wash up.
They look in the mirror.

26

April laughs.

Now Mae laughs, too.

"The field *was* muddy," says Mae.

"*So* muddy," says April.

"And we *do* look funny," says Mae.

"*So* funny," says April.

When they are all washed up,
April and Mae eat a snack.
It is *so* good.
"Mmmm," says April.

"Maybe I am not *that*
bad at soccer," says Mae.
"You are not," says April.

"Maybe it is *mud* that is
bad for soccer," says Mae.
"It is," says April.
"But mud is good for laughs."
"So are you," says Mae.
"Thanks," says April.
"I try."

Now Mae is not sad.
She is glad.
And so is April.
She makes up a new cheer.
"Do you want to hear my cheer?"
April asks.
"Yes," says Mae.

April cheers,

*"It's OK to lose a match!
We can still have
yummy snacks!*

*It's OK to get all muddy!
We can still laugh
with a buddy!*

Best. Friend. GOALS!"

"You are the best!" says Mae.

"Thanks," says April.

  Mae bites into another snack.

"Maybe next time we will win," says April.

"Maybe," says Mae.

"But guess what?"

"What?" asks April.

"I missed a soccer goal," says Mae.

"But we are *best friend* goals."

"Yes!" says April.
"And our pets are, too."

April and Mae look at their pets.
April's dog is trying
to wash Mae's cat.
Mae's cat is trying
to wash April's dog.

"They take care of each other," says Mae.
"That's what friends are for," says April.
"But I think they need help," says Mae.
"I think you're right," says April.

Now the pets are all clean.

Now snack time is over.
Now the friends say goodbye.

"Ta-ta," says Mae.

"Toodles," says April.

"The End," says this book.